This book belong

_____

Series title: Fables from Around the World

ISBN: 978-1-942214-10-6
Adapted by Ronan Keane
Illustrations by Sasa Gvozdenovic
Design by Tseng Yu-Ting

www.rindle-books.com

The Baboon
and
the Tortoise

One evening, Thabo was walking home when he met Bosede.

"Good evening!" said the baboon. "Have you had dinner yet?"

"No," the tortoise sadly replied.

Thabo was very grateful ... but he didn't notice Bosede's sneaky smirk.

Bosede bounced off, and Thabo followed as fast as he could.

"Wait for me!" Thabo called, but he quickly fell behind.

It was a long way to Bosede's house, but Thabo plodded on, thinking happily about the meal awaiting him.

Finally he reached the tree where Bosede had made his home.

"That took you a long time!" said the baboon.

"Oh well, at least I had time to prepare supper. Look, your plate is set."

Poor Thabo craned his neck in the direction the baboon was pointing and saw that a table had in fact been set ... but he knew he could never reach it.

"Can you bring my plate down? Let's eat on the ground," he suggested.

"Nonsense!" Bosede said. "Anyone who wants to eat with me must be able to climb."

Then he burst into laughter and started eating on his own. As Thabo turned around and began the long walk home, he could still hear Bosede laughing.

A few days later, Bosede received a letter. It was from Thabo—an invitation to eat with him that evening.

Bosede was surprised, but also delighted, and set off right away.

It was the dry season, and there had recently been a fire near where Thabo lived.

Bosede could see Thabo cooking and setting a table, but to reach him, he had to cross a patch of ground that was scorched and black.

"Ah, my friend Bosede," said Thabo, "I'm so glad you could make it. But oh no, your hands are all dirty. I can't let you eat without washing them first."

"Let's use the water in this bucket to wash our hands," Bosede suggested.

"There isn't enough for both of us," said Thabo, "and I'll need to wash my own hands. Go and wash your hands in the stream while I finish cooking."

Bosede scampered to the stream to wash his hands, but on his way back, he had to cross the same patch of black ground.

When he returned to the table, his hands were as dirty as before.

Thabo had already started eating. "Let me see your hands," he said between mouthfuls.

"They're still dirty! Go wash them again!"

Bosede went back to the stream, and he decided to take the long way back so he could avoid the scorched ground. But the long way was very muddy.

"Eww!" said the tortoise. "They look worse than they did before! Go back and wash them properly this time!"

Again and again, the baboon went back to the stream, but each time he got his hands dirty on his way back.

Meanwhile, the tortoise kept eating and eating ... and soon there was no food left.

Finally, hungry and tired, Bosede walked back to his tree. He no longer thought it was fun to play tricks on the other animals.

What you do comes back to you.

FABLES FROM AROUND THE WORLD SERIES